Molly & Family!

:I hope you love the book!

[signature]

WILLIAM THE DINOSAUR

MATTHEW VAN KLEECK
ILLUSTRATED BY STAN MOHR

Outskirts Press, Inc.
http://www.outskirtspress.com

ISBN: 978-1-4787-7390-0

Outskirts Press and the "OP" logo are trademarks belonging to Outskirts Press, Inc.

PRINTED IN THE UNITED STATES OF AMERICA

DENVER, COLORADO

This Book Belongs to:

William the Dinosaur,
what a scary sight!
He is ferocious in the morning!

He is ferocious in the night!

He romps and stomps and grumbles.
He rumbles and he roars!
He is quite the fearsome creature,
William the Dinosaur!

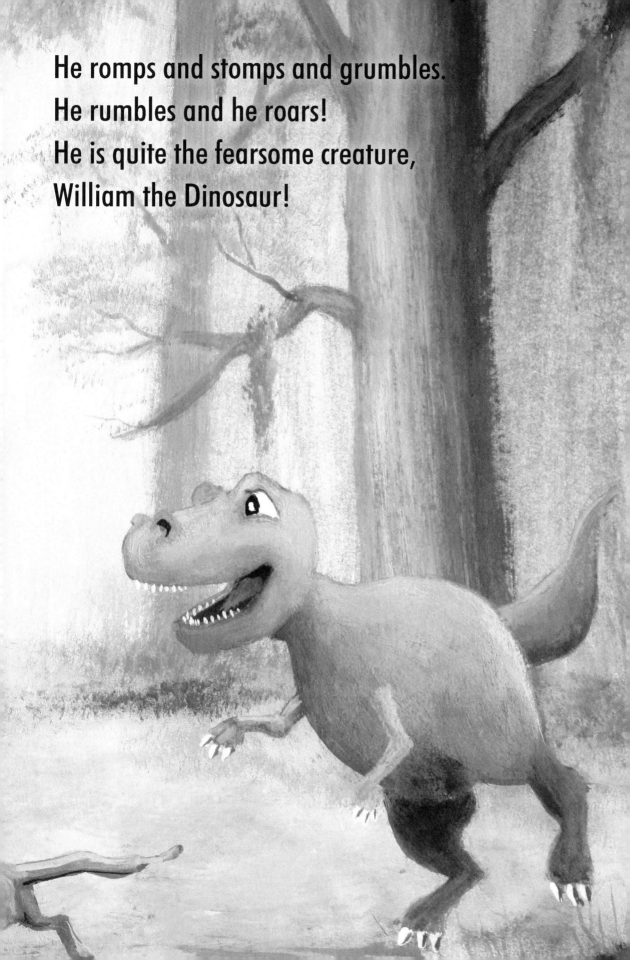

But William loves his mommy.

He is kind to other creatures.

He hugs his Dino Daddy.

He listens to his teachers.

And when his little sister
comes stomping up to play
and asks him for his favorite toy,
he sweetly growls, "You may."

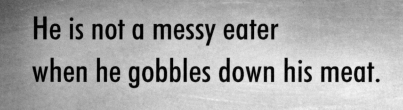

He is not a messy eater
when he gobbles down his meat.

He asks for things politely
and sits nicely in his seat.

When the rainy season comes
and William gets a bath
he does not whine or mumble,
he just jumps in with a laugh.

And when the bright moon rises
above the jungle trees
Mommy and Daddy Dino
tuck him in beneath the leaves.

Then William folds his little hands
and says a little prayer.
He snuggles up all safe and warm
and cozy in his lair.

He is fierce and ferocious,
but, oh, so well behaved!
He is William the sweet dinosaur.
He is loving, kind and brave.